*By turning the page, I, the reader of this book, solemnly swear to follow the factory rules. I will not make a mess. I will not bring colors into the factory. I will not initiate or participate in any surprises.

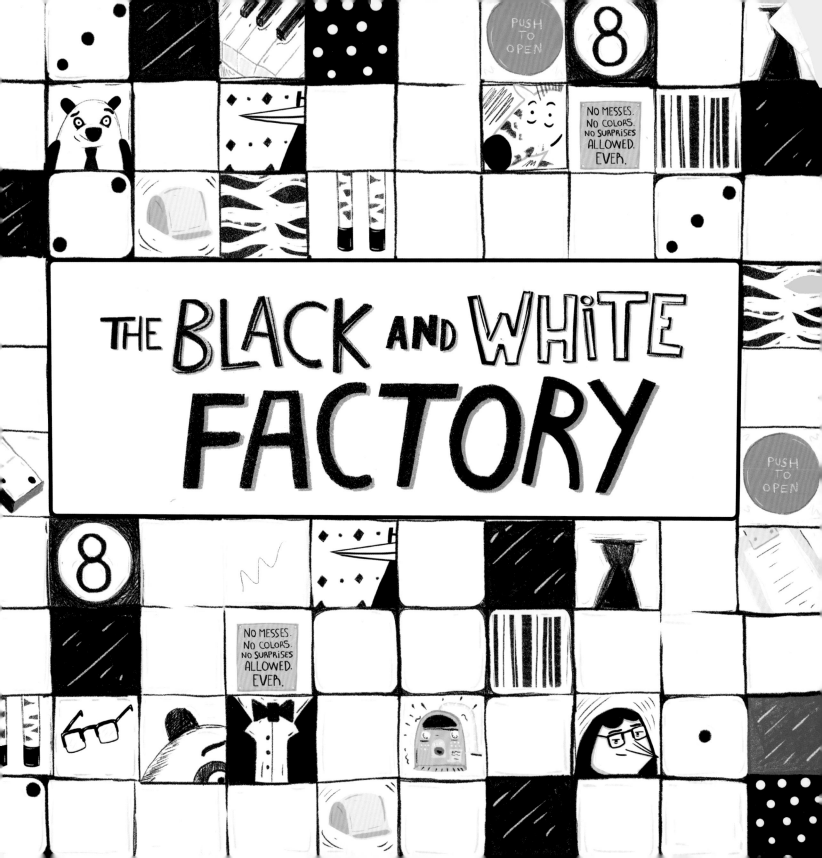

For my brothers and sisters—
Jamie, Jessica, Lauren, and Brian
—E.T.

To Nadia, who loves my
messes, colors, and surprises
—D.F.

New York, New York
Text copyright © 2016, 2021 by Eric Telchin
Illustrations copyright © 2016, 2021 by Little Bee Books
Manufactured in China   RRD 0721
First Edition
2 4 6 8 10 9 7 5 3 1
Library of Congress Cataloging-in-Publication Data
is available upon request.
ISBN 978-1-4998-1347-0

littlebeebooks.com
For information about special discounts on bulk purchases, please
contact Little Bee Books at sales@littlebeebooks.com.

THE BLACK AND WHITE FACTORY

by ERIC TELCHIN   ILLUSTRATED by DIEGO FUNCK

little bee books

BLACK AND WHITE FACTO
Hello. And congratulations! You've just won a tour of the top-secret Black and White Factory.
Everything we make here is black and white. Checkerboards, dice, tuxedos… Even *we* are black and white!

PLAYING
CARDS
EIGHT BALLS
SALT & PEPPER
TOP SECRET
EXPERIMENT ROOM
CHESS PIECES
TUXEDOS
TOP-SELLING BLACK AND WHITE PRODUCTS
OPEN
Now let's take a peek inside the top-secret Experiment Room.

TOP SECRET EXPERIMENT ROOM

PROJECTS:

NEVER-MELTING VANILLA ICE-CREAM

NO MESSES. NO COLORS. NO SURPRISES ALLOWED. EVER.

Look at all the exciting black and white products we're developing in the top-secret Experiment Room. For example, these trick dominoes are impossible to knock over.

CHECKERED PAINT

POLKA DOT PAINT

And our black and white paint is available in either checkered or polka dot.

TRICK DOMINOES

R-POWERED COMPREHENSIVE CLEANING CONTRAPTION
NOZZLE
FOR EMERGENCIES ONLY. INSTRUCTIONS: BLOW AIR INTO THE NOZZLE TO START CONTRAPTION.
ANIMAL ROOM
PUSH TO OPEN
But there's even more through the next door! When you're ready, press the buzzer to move on to the Animal Room.
SELF-ROLLING DICE
DRIP-RESISTANT FUDGE

Welcome to the Bar Code Room—the cleanest, most perfect, most black and white room in the whole factory.
Every bar code in the world is made right here. Even *this* book has one! Turn the book over to the back cover and see for yourself!
MESSES.
COLORS.
SURPRISES
ALLOWED.
EVER.
BAR CODE STAMPER
978 1 4998 0277 1
978 1 4998 0277 1

Wait! Don't go any further! How did *color* get inside our perfectly clean factory?
Someone didn't follow the rules. Someone brought an outside mess into the Black and White Factory.
Could you help us? Use your fingers to wipe the color off the bar code. Go on, put some muscle into it!

Quick! Do something!
Rub the colors with your sleeve.
Or your elbow.
Something.

NO MESSES.
NO COLORS.
NO SURPRISES
ALLOWED
EVER.
We can’t have any color in the Black and White Factory!

I've got an idea. Hold the book upright and tilt it so the color drips down the bottom of the page.

Nice job! You made the color drip out of the book. The factory is spotless again.

Uh-oh. Now there are more colors creeping in from all that tilting!
There's only one way to fix this. Swirl the book in a circle so the colors fly off the page.

We've got one more possible solution. Quick! Back to the top-secret Experiment Room.

If there's one thing that might be able to clean up our big, terrible mess, it's this machine.
AIR-POWERED COMPREHENSIVE CLEANING CONTRAPTION
NOZZLE
FOR EMERGENCIES ONLY. INSTRUCTIONS: BLOW AIR INTO THE NOZZLE TO START CONTRAPTION

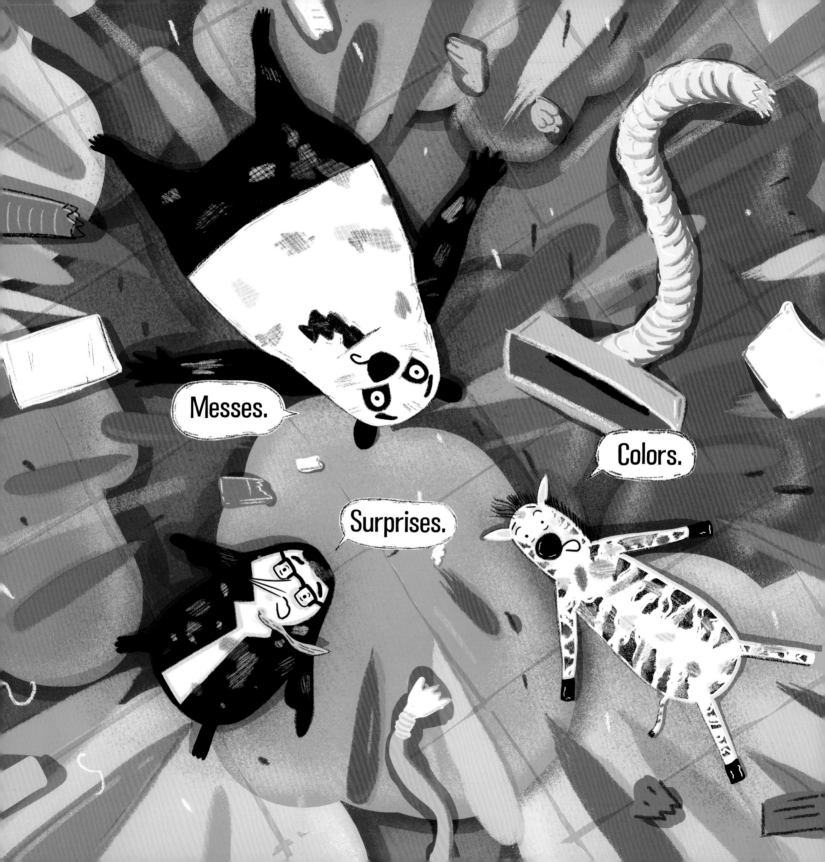

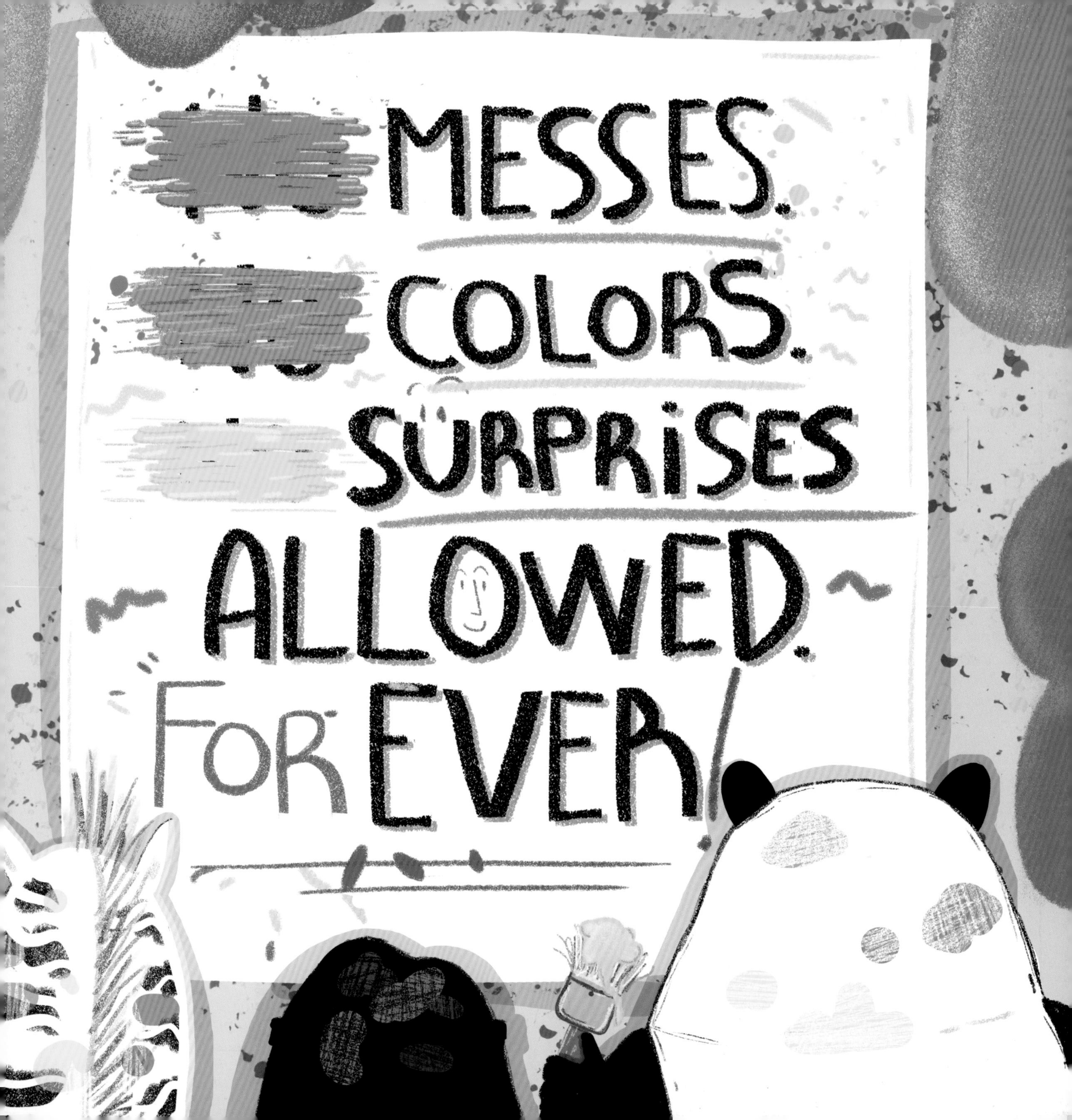
MESSES.
COLORS.
SURPRISES
ALLOWED.
FOREVER!

Eric Telchin grew up in Niskayuna, New York, and graduated magna cum laude from George Washington University. He worked in design at ABC News and at washingtonpost.com before creating Boy Sees Hearts, which showcases photographs of naturally occurring heart shapes, and writing the book *See a Heart, Share a Heart*, as well as *The Black and White Factory*. He currently lives in West Palm Beach, Florida.

Diego Funck is an illustrator and graphic designer from Buenos Aires, Argentina, and is the illustrator of *The Black and White Factory*. He's been drawing professionally for the past twelve years, creating children's books and working with educational publishers in Belgium, Congo, Haiti, and India. He currently lives in Brussels, Belgium.

ON
Reader! Turn the power back on! Now we don't need to close the Color Factory!
These colors are factory approved!

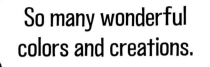

Uh-oh . . .
Now there are even *more* non-factory-approved colors!
NOT FACTORY APPROVED
We'll have to check the *Color Manual* again to find a solution.

ADDING COLOR
TO THE COLOR FACTORY:

If you removed factory-approved colors from the Color Factory, you're in big, BIG trouble. You better ask someone for help!

INSTRUCTIONS:
CLEANING
NON-FACTORY-APPROVED COLORS FROM THE COLOR FACTORY

You're in big trouble! To remove non-factory-approved colors from the factory, you had better ask someone for help!

?

S.O.S.

COLOR MANUAL

iNDEX

- Chameleons

- Cleaning Non-Factory-Approved Colors from the Color Factory

- Creature Colorization Complications (see also: Chameleons)

- Discontinued Colors (see also: Factory-Approved Purple)

- Dots, Stripes, Spirals, and Other Terrifying Things

- Factory-Approved Purple (see also: Discontinued Colors; the Grape Jelly Incident)

PUSH HERE FOR INSTRUCTIONS

Quick! Push the button!

PERFE
COLOR
Uh-oh . . .
Now it's worse! This non-factory-approved color is changing everything!
COLOR MANU
Don't worry. The *Color Manual* will tell us what to do.

NOT FACTORY APPROVED
This color is not in the *Color Manual*! It's not a factory-approved color!
WHE
EEEE
COLOR MANUAL

Use your finger to pull Factory-Approved Robin's Egg Blue onto it. And drag some Factory-Approved Cotton Candy Pink, too.
Be careful not to mix the colors as you apply them to the lollipop! This is very important!

Since you're doing such a perfect job, we'd like you to color this lollipop.

The Confectionary Room is the most colorful, most delicious, most *perfect* room in the whole Color Factory.
3-D ICE-CREAM PRINTER
But we have treats that still need to be colored.
Could you help us?

This egg needs to be colored with Factory-Approved Robin's Egg Blue.
But first we need to mix that color. Simply follow the formula from the *Color Manual*: three taps of Factory-Approved Sky Blue, a quick rub of Factory-Approved Grass Green, and a squiggle of Factory-Approved Cloud White.
PRESS HERE
PERFEC
ICATO
Use your finger to tap, rub, and squiggle. Then press this button.

Perfect! Great job! We approve! The formula for Factory-Approved Orange works every time.
That's because our formulas are perfect!
Because our colors are perfect! Now let's move on to the Creature Colorization Room.

PRESS HERE
Simply tap each color once. Then press this button, please.
PERFECT COLOR REPLICATOR

That's right! Factory-Approved Orange is made from Fire Engine Red and Canary Yellow.
Now that the Perfect Color Replicator has matched these two colors, we just need to mix them together. Can you help us?

And remember those fast-growing rose seeds? Well, they certainly did grow fast. We're copying their color to make Factory-Approved Rose.
Next, we're going to create Factory-Approved Orange. You can probably guess how we're going to do that!

This Perfect Color Replicator machine allows us to calculate an object's exact color ingredients. For example, we just matched the color of this chocolate bar to make Factory-Approved Chocolate Brown.
PRESS HERE
PERFECT COLOR REPLICATOR
SCANNING
PROCESSING
OBJECT I.D: CHOCOLATE
CREATION

We create colors here.
We use very strict formulas so we can make these colors *perfect*.
Once the colors are approved, we apply them to all sorts of things!
We also make books!
In fact, the book you're reading *right now* is filled with factory-approved colors.
Simply turn the page and we'll start the tour!
FAST-GROWING ROSE SEEDS
Factory-Approved Rose
18 COLORS
Factory-Approved Canary Yellow

For the most colorful people I know, my nieces
and nephews: Marly, Derek, Brooke, Henry, and Oliver
—ET

To Julen
—DF

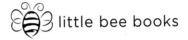

New York, New York
Text copyright ©2016, 2021 by Eric Telchin
Illustrations copyright © 2016, 2021 by Little Bee Books
Manufactured in China   RRD 0721
First Edition
2 4 6 8 10 9 7 5 3 1
Library of Congress Cataloging-in-Publication Data
is available upon request.
ISBN 978-1-4998-1347-0
littlebeebooks.com
For information about special discounts on bulk purchases, please
contact Little Bee Books at sales@littlebeebooks.com.

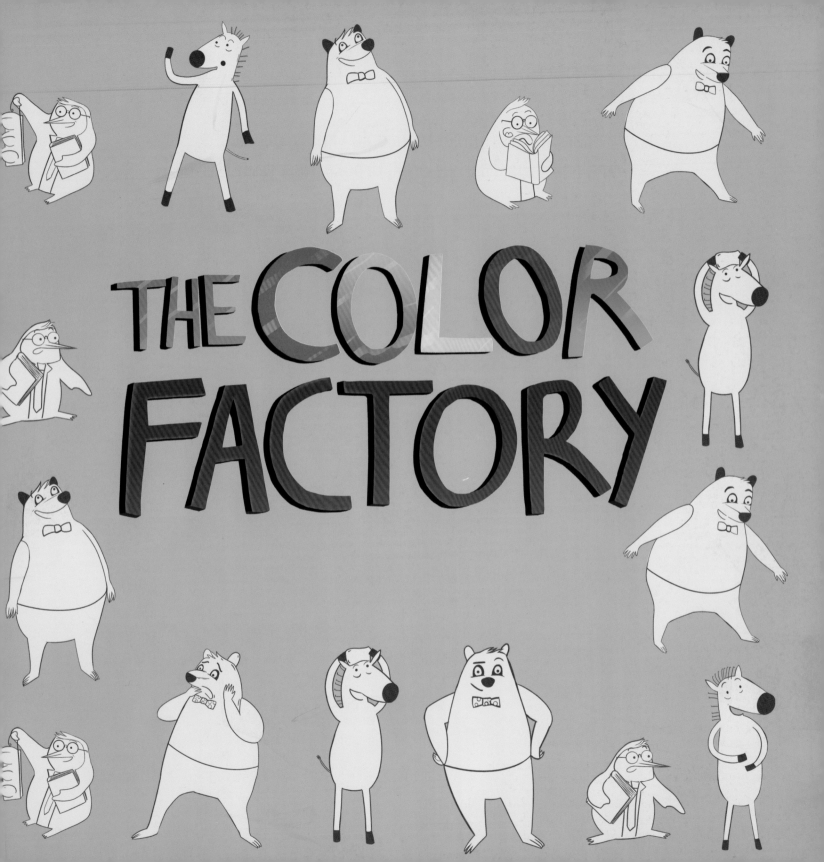